A PARRAGON BOOK
Published by Parragon Book Service Ltd, Unit 13-17 Avonbridge Trading Estate,
Atlantic Road, Avonmouth, Bristol BS11 9QD
Produced by The Templar Company plc, Pippbrook Mill,
London Road, Dorking, Surrey RH4 1JE
Printed and bound in Italy
ISBN 0-75250-877-6

PICTURE TALES

The Pied Piper

Illustrated by Tom Pepperday

·PARRAGON·

Once upon a time, in a town

called Hamelin, there was a

terrible plague of . They

came to eat the , which

the town produced. But in

addition they fought the ,

7

killed the , bit the

in their , ate and

, and nested in the men's

best . They squeaked

and squealed, until the

townsfolk were deafened.

9

After months of misery the decided to take action.

They demanded that the mayor find a way to rid the  of the , or else they would get rid of him!

So the sent out a

proclamation offering a

to anyone who could rid the

town of . Next day a

strange in a long red

and yellow appeared .

13

Around his neck was a ,
and he wore a with a red
. He told the he could
free the town of the ,
with a secret charm, and said
his name was the Pied Piper.

The  was delighted, and

promised not one, but

if the could rid the

 of . So the

 went into the ,

and put the to his .

Before he had played three , there came a rumbling as poured out into the , and followed the and his magic . He led them to the , where they plunged in

one by one and drowned. Soon

all the were dead and the

people rejoiced in the 🏘 .

Thinking they were safe, the

greedy 👒 refused to pay the

 his 💵 , but offered

him instead. But the

warned he would play a tune of

a different kind if the

was not paid. The

laughed, and invited him to

take up his and play.

So, once more the stepped into the . Before he had played three there was a stirring in the , and all the and from the came through the

and ran after him as he led them

to the . The townsfolk

looked on in horror. But when

the reached the

he turned towards the .

The townsfolk thought he

would never climb it. But then

a appeared in the hillside, and the led the through it. The shut tight behind them, and from that day on, the were never seen in Hamelin again.